TIME TO EAT

ANIMALS WHO HIDE AND SAVE THEIR FOOD

written by
Marilyn Baillie

illustrated by
Romi Caron

Owl Books

Owl Books are published by Greey de Pencier Books Inc.,
179 John Street, Suite 500, Toronto, Ontario M5T 3G5

OWL and the Owl colophon are trademarks of Owl Communications.
Greey de Pencier Books Inc. is a licensed user of trademarks of Owl Communications.

Distributed in the United States by Firefly Books (U.S.) Inc.,
230 Fifth Avenue, Suite 1607, New York, NY 10001.

This book was published with the generous support of the Canada Council, the Ontario Arts Council
and the Government of Ontario through the Ontario Publishing Centre.

Consultant
Dr. Katherine E. Wynne-Edwards, PhD, Biology Dept., Queen's University, Kingston, Ontario

Dedication
For Charles, Matthew, Jonathan and Alexandra with love.

Author's Acknowledgements
A special thank-you to Dr. Katherine Wynne-Edwards for her expertise and generous assistance.
A big thank-you to Editor-in-Chief Sheba Meland and editor Kat Mototsune for their energy and enthusiasm,
to Julia Naimska for her creative design and to Romi Caron for her engaging illustrations.

Canadian Cataloguing in Publication Data

Baillie, Marilyn
Time to eat : animals who hide and save
their food

ISBN 1-895688-36-1 (bound) ISBN 1-895688-30-2 (pbk.)

1. Animals - Food - Juvenile literature. 2. Animal
behavior - Juvenile literature. 3. Animals -
Juvenile literature. I. Caron, Romi. II. Title

QL756.5.B34 1994   j591.5'3   C94-932293-8

Design & Art Direction: Julia Naimska

Photo credits: p. 6 Tom Wiewandt/DRK Photo; p. 8 Partrige Films/Animals, Animals/O.S.F.;
p. 10 Herman H. Giethoorn/Valan; p. 12 Stephen Pruett-Jones; p. 14 Dick Haneda;
p. 16 Raymond Mendez/Animals, Animals; p. 18 John Shaw/Bruce Coleman; p. 20 Stephen J. Krasemann/Valan;
p. 22 Wayne Lankinen/Bruce Coleman; p. 24 Ian Murphy/Tony Stone Images; p. 26 Bill Ivy;
p. 28 J.A. Wilkinson/Valan; pp. 30 – 31 as above.

Printed in Hong Kong

A   B   C   D   E   F

CONTENTS

HIDE AND FIND

We keep our food in cupboards and refrigerators. Animals all over the world store and save their food, too. Animals hide and save food for times when they will really need it. They keep meals ready to eat when food can't be found. Some creatures use many hiding places, and others put all their food in one place. Animals sometimes hide food to keep it safe from scavengers, other animals that like to steal a free meal.

Have you ever wrapped a sandwich to keep it fresh until lunchtime? The garden spider wraps silken threads around a bug to save it for later. The great horned owl doesn't need a freezer for its dinner, or an oven to thaw it. It uses cold winter air and the heat from its own body.

We keep forgetting where we put the ketchup! But little birds called chickadees hide hundreds of tiny seeds, and know exactly where to find each one again. The chickadees here have plucked and hidden lots of seeds to eat later. How many seeds can you see? (You can check how well you did on page 32.) Now, turn the page to meet more animals that store and save their food in amazing ways.

BIG CHEEKS

Daytime is scorching in the desert, but night brings the cool and dark. Once the sun sets, the kangaroo rat hops warily from beneath the sand and scrub to gather seeds. Using her front paws, she neatly packs the seeds into her cheek pockets. Bigger and bigger her cheeks bulge with food. Then . . . hop, hop, the kangaroo rat disappears into her burrow.

The kangaroo rat hurries down deep underground to her nest. There she turns her cheek pockets inside out to empty out every last seed. She sorts the seeds into piles — the small seeds here, the big ones there. Then she hops back into the night for another load.

Soon the desert will get hotter and drier. But the kangaroo rat can stay cool day after day in her underground nest. She won't need to go out for food and water. Her stored seeds give her all the food and liquid she needs. When the hottest season passes, she will leave her burrow again, to gather and hide away seeds.

SAFE ACORNS

Rat-a-tat-tat! What's that sound? An acorn woodpecker is pecking a hole in a hollow tree. Back and forth bobs his head as he chisels with his long, strong beak. Another woodpecker comes to take her turn at the hole. Then a third one arrives. They take turns pecking and tapping, hammering and rapping at the tree trunk until the hole is just the right size and shape.

A woodpecker flies up with an acorn it has plucked from an oak tree. It stuffs it into the new hole. Hundreds of acorns dot the tree, snug in the notches the woodpeckers have made. If any of the acorns dry up and shrink, the woodpeckers pull them out and wedge them into smaller holes made to fit.

There is enough food here for this woodpecker family group to eat all through the bad weather when food is hard to find. The acorns fit tightly in the holes. Only the sharp-beaked woodpeckers can pry the precious food out. These birds jealously guard their acorns. Any animal who tries to snatch one gets shooed away!

BUG BUNDLE

Look in the raspberry bushes — there's a garden spider on her lacy web. Woven between the stems like a net, the long silk strands of the web have trapped a fly for the spider to eat. The garden spider is spinning her silk. She bundles up the tasty fly in the strong thin threads. She will save this wrapped-up meal for later, dangling the bug bundle from a long strand attached to the web.

How does the spider catch her food? Let's watch and see. Here comes a grasshopper. Thud! It bumps into the web and gets stuck on the sticky silk. Its wiggling makes the web shake, so the spider knows another meal has arrived. The spider picks her way across the web on special threads that are not sticky. She bites her prey to make it hold still while she wraps her silk around it and hangs it up. Then she fixes her web and hangs upside-down near the center, waiting for the next insect to come by.

But her silk-wrapped meals are not always safe. The male garden spider is smaller than she is, and he's a clever thief. He patiently waits on a nearby leaf while the female spider traps and wraps her prey. Then he sneaks up and snips his free meal from the web. He slowly lowers the bundle to the ground on a hanging thread, and carries it away!

HANDY SNACKS

Fresh figs and other fruits fill the tree branches. But here's a mystery — these fruits didn't grow on these trees. Who put all this fruit here? It was the MacGregor's bowerbird. He has propped juicy fruits in the forks of tree branches, keeping it handy and ready to eat. It's mating season and he has a lot of work to do — no time to fly around and look for food.

The bowerbird piles and fits bits of twigs together around a sapling. Slowly, a tall tower shape grows. He carefully lays a covering of soft moss around the bottom. This is not a nest he's building. It's called a bower, and it's a special place for him to show off to a female bird.

When the bower is finished and he has filled the trees with fresh fruit, the bowerbird is ready. He sees a female bird, and starts to dance around his bower on the moss. Look at his bright orange crest! What a beautiful bower! Surely a new mate will want to come and stay a while?

Up a Tree

The quiet of the African plain is hardly broken by the crack of a branch. In the faint evening light, a spotted shadow slips to the ground from an acacia tree. It's a leopard. She slinks towards a grazing herd of gazelles, and then she pauses, still and silent. Suddenly, with one swift pounce, the leopard catches her supper. The rest of the gazelles bound away.

A pack of hyenas lurks in the grass, watching the leopard eat her supper and hoping to steal the leftovers. She can't keep these scavengers away all by herself. How will she protect the rest of her food?

The leopard grasps the gazelle with her strong jaws and drags the heavy load to a tree. Her sharp claws dig deep into the tree trunk as she hauls up her catch. The leopard slings her food over a sturdy tree branch safe from the hyenas, who can't climb. Then she stretches out on a nearby limb to catnap and keep watch. Now, who would dare steal food from the mighty leopard?

Hanging Honeypots

Home, sweet home for honeypot ants is this nest under the ground. What are those roly-poly balls on the ceiling? The balls are special honeypot ants, puffed up to about eight times their usual size! Each ant is full of stored plant nectar and honeydew, like a balloon filled with sugary water. The storage ants can't move much, so worker ants bring them food and keep them full to bursting.

During the dry season, plants wither. There is no nectar in the plants for the worker ants to eat. That's when they get food from their roly-poly friends. Gently they stroke the storage ants with their antennae. The storage ants drop liquid food from their mouths for the hungry workers to sip. The whole nest can live for many months through a dry spell, all thanks to the honeypot storage ants.

Cool Treats

Far above the ground, the great horned owl sits still as the cold night air. Suddenly — whir-r-r-r! — his wide wings softly cut through the darkness. He swoops down, following a mouse running across the frozen meadow. He snatches the mouse with his needle-sharp talons and flies back to his perch. He stores his catch in a fork of the tree, where it quickly freezes in the wintry air.

Nearby, the owl's mate snuggles down over her two eggs, keeping them warm and safe. She can't leave the nest when she is hungry, so her mate will feed her. Since the mouse is frozen like an ice cube, the male owl has to melt it somehow. He sits on the mouse, and the warmth of his body thaws it. Now he can give his mate a delicious defrosted treat.

PILED HIGH

It's harvest time! A pika scurries by with a mouthful of fresh grass. He tosses his bundle onto a big stack of shoots and grasses, and then disappears to find more. All day long the pika adds to his tall haystack. Among the green and brown stems and leaves are bright flowers — the blossoms of yellow alpine arnica, Red Indian Paintbrush and blue harebells.

The pika's haystack is already as big as the huge boulders on the mountain slope. Sometimes he spreads grass on the rocks to dry in the late summer sun before moving it to his pile. Why? Like a farmer, he knows the sun-dried food will keep well over the winter months.

Through the winter, the pika will search for lichens, bark and roots in the snow. But when a winter storm blows in, this wise little mountain animal can feed on the plants he piled high for those blustery days.

HIDE AND SEEK

Chickadee-dee-dee! The chickadee chirps her name as she hunts for food, even after she has eaten. She finds a tiny seed and flies off with it cupped in her beak. She tucks this treasure into the crevice of a tree. She hides another seed in a hollow stem nearby. She finds and hides seed after seed. Such an active little bird will need all these small meals later.

Will the chickadee be able to find all her secret hiding spots? When she returns, she suddenly darts towards the tree crevice. The seed is right there! The chickadee flits from hiding place to hiding place, finding every hidden seed. She remembers the way the hiding spots look and returns to them one by one.

In northern areas, chickadees hide seeds in the fall to eat during the winter. Weeks after hiding their food, these little birds remember where it is hidden . . . even if a snowfall has blanketed the trees and changed the autumn forest to winter white!

SOAKING WET

Two bulging eyes and a round snout poke out of the murky river. A crocodile is floating just below the surface of the water like a bumpy old log. Silent and still, he watches a thirsty water buffalo come to the river's edge. When it bends down to lap some water, Snap! The crocodile's jaws open and close like giant scissors. He pulls his dinner into the river.

The crocodile is hungry, but he has to wait. His long, sharp teeth are good for grasping but not as good for chewing. The tough meat has to soften in the water before he can eat it. The crocodile drags his meal to a hole in the muddy river bank. It is the perfect place to keep the food for a few days until it is nice and tender. The water will hide the meat from the vultures. It will wash away the smell that would bring other animals to steal his dinner. Patiently, the crocodile floats nearby, waiting for his feast.

A Sweet Team

Bzzzzzzzz, Bzzzzzzzz! Honeybees burst into the hive with the good news. Pollen and nectar! But in which direction? How far away? The bees start to dance and their hive mates crowd around. Bees who have found new flowers full of food dance this special waggle dance. It tells other bees where to collect the pollen and nectar to bring back to the hive.

The hive is home to the whole colony. This is where the bees keep the food they gather. All the honeybees work together to keep their honey safe and fresh.

After worker bees have collected nectar, other bees in the hive dry the nectar into honey. To keep it from spoiling, they mix in preservatives they make in their bodies. Then they store the honey in honeycombs. Guard bees buzz around outside. They attack and sting any stranger, from the smallest ant to the biggest bear, that tries to steal the sweet honey from the hive.

WOOD FOR WINTER

Back and forth the beavers swim, dragging branches and twigs in their mouths. This family has work to finish before winter comes. They use their large front teeth to cut down trees, gnawing and chopping. Stick by stick, they build their house, or lodge, from the tougher branches. They will live all winter in their lodge, right in the middle of the frozen pond covered with snow.

The beavers save the tenderest branches for their winter food supply. They store tasty twigs inside the warm, dry lodge. They pile more food in a huge underwater mound, jamming big branches into the muddy pond bottom and stuffing smaller twigs in between. The pile grows until it reaches all the way to the surface of the pond. When the pond freezes over, the best pieces will be beneath the ice, easy to pull out and drag home.

All through the winter, the beaver family will munch on the food they've collected. When all the twigs in their lodge are gone, the beavers will swim under the frozen surface of the pond to the big pile of food just outside their door! Just like carrot sticks sitting in water in your fridge, the twigs stay juicy and crisp in the icy cold pond.

WHO'S WHO

KANGAROO RAT

Kangaroo rats live in dry scrub and desert areas through North, Central and northern South America. The kangaroo rat is a bit bigger than a mouse. Its oversized back legs and a tail that is three times the length of its body give it the strength and balance to jump several times its own height.

MACGREGOR'S BOWERBIRD

Most bowerbirds live in northern Australia, but MacGregor's bowerbird lives in the lush mountain forests of New Guinea. It is about the same size as a North American robin. Each bowerbird has its own unique bower design to attract females and sometimes to display food and treasures.

ACORN WOODPECKER

Acorn woodpeckers live in large family groups in the wooded foothills and mixed forests of southwestern North America, and further south into the tropics. The length of your forearm from your elbow to your wrist is about how high an acorn woodpecker would stand.

LEOPARD

Leopards live in the rainforests, deserts, mountains or lowland plains of Asia and Africa. Now only a few leopards are left since they have been hunted for their beautiful spotted fur. A leopard is about the size of a big dog, but is muscular, very sleek, and extremely powerful.

GARDEN SPIDER

Garden spiders live worldwide except in Antarctica. Not all kinds of spiders spin webs, but garden spiders are part of the large group that do. Look among plants and you might recognize a web and a waiting spider with thread-thin legs and a body about the size of the tip of your thumb.

HONEYPOT ANTS

Honeypot ants live in dry areas of Australia, North America and Africa. Underground nests are divided into "galleries": nurseries near the surface where it is warm, and food stores deeper where it is cool. Repletes or storage ants swell from the size of a grain of sand to the size of a pea.

GREAT HORNED OWL

Great horned owls live in the wooded and open areas of North, Central and South America. They often hatch their eggs in nests that have been built and abandoned by other birds. Listen for a low "Hoot, hoot, hoot, hoot," and look for a large bird with wings that open about as far as an adult's outstretched arms.

CROCODILE

Crocodiles live in the rivers, lakes and swamps of tropical regions all over the world. The ancestors of today's crocodiles lived at the time of the dinosaurs and were about the length of a school bus. Now crocodiles are only car-length but, like their relatives, they have huge, powerful jaws that can snap shut like a steel trap.

PIKA

In grassy nests cradled between the rocks, pikas live in the Rocky Mountains of western North America and in mountains throughout Asia. If you see one, it will be a furry animal the size of a small guinea pig scurrying amongst the boulders or running on top of the snow. If you hear a short, sharp whistle, you'll know that it's a pika.

HONEYBEE

Wild honeybees build nests in holes of trees or in rocky openings in temperate and tropical regions of Europe, Asia, North America and Africa. People throughout the world keep honeybees for the use of their delicious honey. If you see a honeybee buzz by, it will be about the size of the metal eraser-holder on the end of a pencil.

CHICKADEE

Chickadees are friendly, living in wooded backyards, parks and forests of North America. Listen for a cheery "chick-a-dee-dee-dee" call and look for a small bird about the size of a child's fist. Expect more than one, since they live in pairs through spring and summer, and start to gather into small flocks in August.

BEAVER

Beavers live in streams, ponds and lakes in the cooler parts of North America and Asia. The beaver is the size of a small dog, with a broad, flat tail and two long, orange front teeth. In the winter, if you pass a lodge of sticks in the middle of a frozen pond, you just might hear the soft sounds of the beavers inside.

WHO AM I?

Here's a quiz for you to try. Each clue tells you how an animal hides or stores its food. Which animal from this book is speaking? Answers are below.

1 A dead tree is like a big cupboard for my family's food.

2 While I look for a mate, I keep a supply of fresh fruit handy in my forest pantry.

3 I catch my food in my strong, scissor-like jaws, and then soak it to make it soft.

4 I'm like a farmer, harvesting grass and piling it in a haystack.

5 I'm a big cat that likes to climb trees, and that's where I drag my food to keep it safe.

6 The frozen water outside my home keeps my meals crisp and juicy.

7 I collect my food in special pockets and take it to my burrow under the desert sand.

8 I dance to tell my friends where they can find food to bring home.

9 I wrap up my meals in individual packages.

10 I hide my food in lots of different places, and remember them all.

11 I use the winter air to freeze my food, and then I defrost it so it's ready to eat.

12 I am like a living food barrel, dangling from the ceiling.

ANSWERS

Hide and Find, pages 4–5

Who Am I?

1. Acorn Woodpecker	6. Beaver
2. MacGregor's Bowerbird	5. Leopard
3. Crocodile	4. Pika
7. Kangaroo Rat	10. Chickadee
8. Honeybee	9. Garden Spider
	11. Great Horned Owl
	12. Honeypot Ant